JUST ME AND MY PUPPY

BY
MERCER MAYER

For Roger Buoy,
who's always wanted
a puppy of his very own.

A Random House PICTUREBACK® Book

Random House New York

 Published in the United States by Random House Children's Books, a division of Random House, Inc., New York. Originally published in 1985 by Golden Books Publishing Company, Inc. PICTUREBACK, RANDOM HOUSE, and the Random House colophon are registered trademarks of Random House, Inc.

www.randomhouse.com/kids

Educators and librarians, for a variety of teaching tools, visit us at www.randomhouse.com/teachers

Library of Congress Control Number: 84-82601

ISBN-13: 978-0-307-11937-7 ISBN-10: 0-307-11937-8

Printed in the United States of America

16 15 14 13 12 11 10 9 8 7

First Random House Edition 2006

I wanted a puppy, just for me.
So I traded my baseball mitt for one.

My baby sister liked him right away.

And, boy, were Mom and Dad surprised! They said I could keep him if I took care of him myself.

So I am taking very good care
of my puppy.
I feed him in the morning.

He eats every bite.

Then I put on his leash and
we go for a walk.

I am teaching my puppy
how to heel.

He is learning how to stay . . .

. . . except when he sees a cat.

My puppy knows lots of tricks . . .

how to sit . . .

how to play dead . . .

. . . and how to roll over.

He still needs some practice.

But he already knows how to fetch.

My puppy is a big help around the house.

He's a good guard dog.

He brings in
the paper
for my dad.

And he keeps me company
while I do my homework.

Sometimes my puppy
gets dirty.

Then I give him a bath.

I get him nice and dry
so he won't catch a cold.

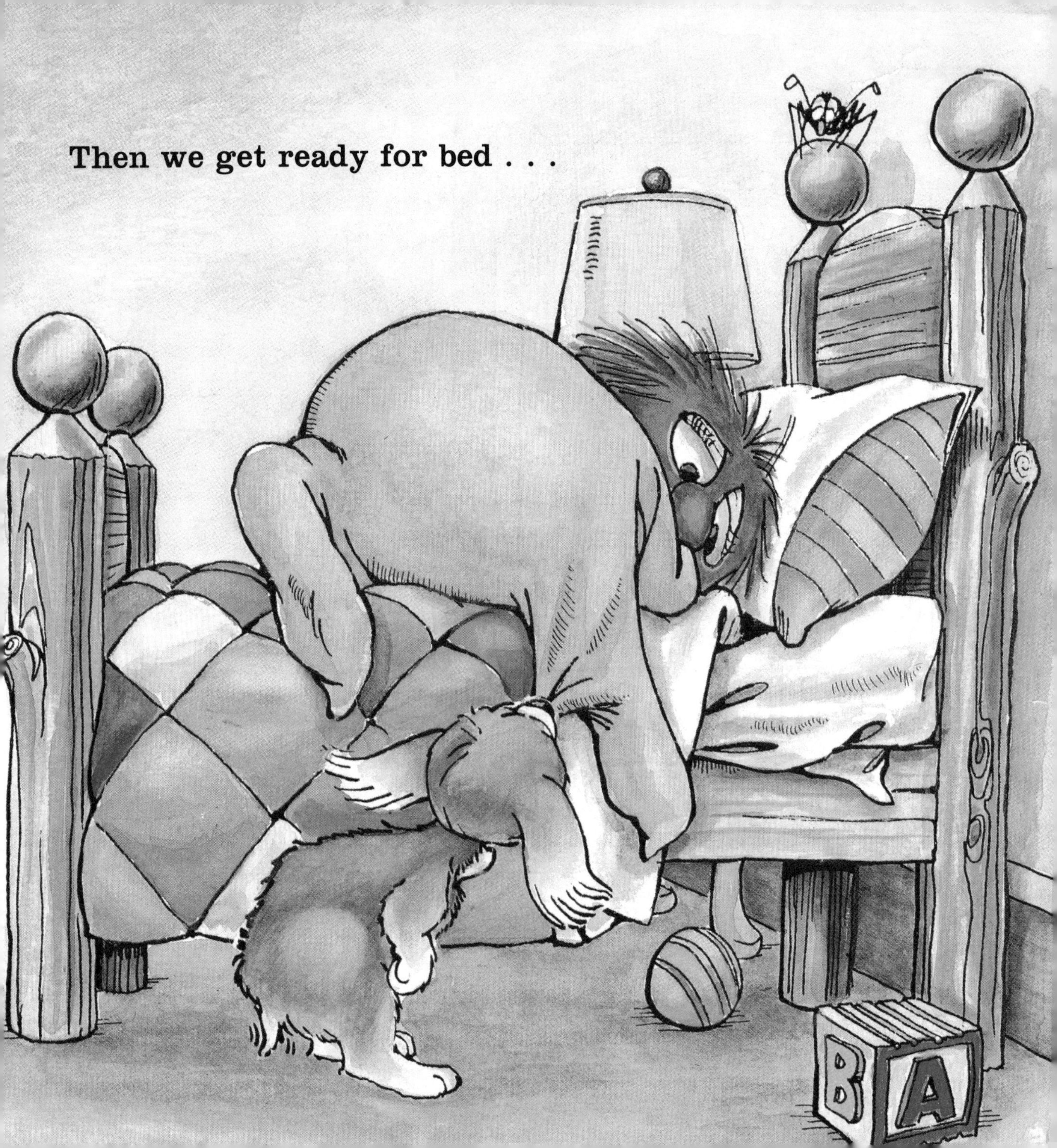

Then we get ready for bed . . .

. . . just me and my puppy.